Katy Duck's
Happy Halloween

By Alyssa Satin Capucilli Illustrated by Henry Cole

Ready-to-Read

Simon Spotlight

New York   London   Toronto   Sydney   New Delhi

For my favorite trick-or-treaters,
Peter, Laura, and Huck!
—A. S. C.

To all those who love Halloween . . .
my favorite holiday!
—H. C.

 SIMON SPOTLIGHT
An imprint of Simon & Schuster Children's Publishing Division
1230 Avenue of the Americas, New York, New York 10020
Text copyright © 2014 by Alyssa Satin Capucilli
Illustrations copyright © 2014 by Henry Cole
All rights reserved, including the right of reproduction in whole or in part in any form.
SIMON SPOTLIGHT, READY-TO-READ, and colophon are registered trademarks of
Simon & Schuster, Inc.
For information about special discounts for bulk purchases, please contact Simon & Schuster
Special Sales at 1-866-506-1949 or business@simonandschuster.com.
The Simon & Schuster Speakers Bureau can bring authors to your live event. For more information or
to book an event contact the Simon & Schuster Speakers Bureau at 1-866-248-3049 or visit our website
at www.simonspeakers.com.
Manufactured in the United States of America 0815 LAK
10 9 8 7 6 5 4
Library of Congress Cataloging-in-Publication Data
Capucilli, Alyssa Satin, 1957–
Katy Duck's happy Halloween / by Alyssa Satin Capucilli ; illustrated by Henry Cole. — First edition.
pages cm — (Ready-to-read)
Summary: "Katy Duck is excited for Halloween. Until she sees Alice Duck dressed up in a shimmery,
glimmery outfit. Katy wishes she was shimmery and glimmery, too. But with a little help from Alice
and Ralph, Katy realizes that her costume is still very special. And besides, she can be shimmery and
glimmery next year"— Provided by publisher.
ISBN 978-1-4424-9806-8 (pbk) — ISBN 978-1-4424-9807-5 (hc) — ISBN 978-1-4424-9808-2 (eBook)
[1. Halloween—Fiction. 2. Costume—Fiction. 3. Ducks—Fiction.] I. Cole, Henry, illustrator. II. Title.
PZ7.C179Ko 2014
[E]—dc23
2013045346

It was Halloween.
Katy Duck could hardly
wait to go trick-or-treating.

"Tra-la-la. Quack! Quack!
I can get ready for
Halloween all by myself,"
said Katy Duck.

Katy dug through
her costume box.

"I will be a dancing unicorn!" said Katy Duck. "No one will have a costume like this."

Katy galloped.

Katy twirled.

Just then the doorbell rang.

It was Ralph!

"Trick-or-treat!" said Ralph.

"Come on, Katy Duck.

We are waiting for you."

Katy Duck fixed her
unicorn wings.
She hurried outside.

"Tra-la-la. Trick-or-treat!"
called Katy Duck.

"Tra-la-la.
Oh my!"

There was Alice Duck.
Alice wore the most
wonderful costume
Katy had ever seen.

Alice
shimmered.

Alice
glimmered.

"Tra-la-la. Boohoo!"
said Katy Duck.
Suddenly she wanted a
costume that shimmered
and glimmered, too.

Katy Duck looked down.
This Halloween was not
much of a treat after all.

"Ready?" asked Ralph.

Katy looked at everyone
in their costumes.
She did not want to
miss Halloween.

Slowly, Katy Duck joined
her friends.
Mrs. Duck took a
picture of the group!

"I like your costume, Katy," said Alice Duck.

"I like yours too, Alice," said Katy Duck. "A lot."

"I want to be a dancing unicorn next Halloween," said Alice.
"But I do not know how."

"Really?" said Katy Duck.

"I can show you how.

It is easy!"

Katy took Alice's hand.

"Ready, set, trick-or-treat!" called Ralph.

Katy Duck and Alice
skipped down the street.

Together, they shimmered
and glimmered.

Together, they galloped
and twirled.

"Tra-la-la. Trick-or-treat! Tra-la-la. Happy Halloween!"